OCT 2008

W9-BYJ-713

Primrose

and
the Magic Snowglobe

J. H. Sweet

Illustrated by Tara Larsen Chang

SOURCEBOOKS
Jabberwocky
AN IMPRINT OF SOURCEBOOKS

© 2008 by J. H. Sweet
Cover and internal design © 2008 by Sourcebooks, Inc.
Cover and internal illustrations © Tara Larsen Chang
Internal photos © Jupiter Images
Sourcebooks and the colophon are registered trademarks of Sourcebooks, Inc.

All rights reserved. No part of this book may be reproduced in any form or by
any electronic or mechanical means including information storage and retrieval
systems—except in the case of brief quotations embodied in critical articles or
reviews—without permission in writing from its publisher, Sourcebooks, Inc.

The characters and events portrayed in this book are fictitious or are used ficti-
tiously. Any similarity to real persons, living or dead, is purely coincidental and
not intended by the author.

What follows is the original, unaltered manuscript directly from the author. It
is her vision in its purest form.

Published by Sourcebooks Jabberwocky, an imprint of
Sourcebooks, Inc.
P.O. Box 4410, Naperville, Illinois 60567-4410
(630) 961-3900
Fax: (630) 961-2168
www.fairychronicles.com

Library of Congress Cataloging-in-Publication Data

Sweet, J. H.
  Primrose and the Magic Snowglobe / J. H. Sweet.
    p. cm. — (The Fairy Chronicles ; bk. 9)
  Summary: When Ripper the gremlin, Bruchard the gargoyle, and Mr. Jones
the dwarf start acting against their magical natures, they seek out the fairies,
who assign Primrose and her fairy friends to discover what has happened.
  ISBN-13: 978-1-4022-1163-8 (pbk.)
  ISBN-10: 1-4022-1163-5 (pbk.)
  [1. Fairies—Fiction. 2. Wishes—Fiction. 3. Magic—Fiction.] I. Title.

PZ7.S9547Pr 2008
[Fic]—dc22

                    2007040773

        Printed and bound in China.
        IM 10 9 8 7 6 5 4 3 2 1

*To Ed,
for being my Wishmaker*

MEET THE

Primrose

Name:
Taylor Buchanan

Fairy Name and Spirit:
Primrose

Wand:
Small, Black Raven Feather

Gift:
Ability to solve mysteries

Mentor:
Mrs. Renquist,
Madam Swallowtail

Snapdragon

Name:
Bettina Gregory

Fairy Name and Spirit:
Snapdragon

Wand:
Spiral-Shaped Black
Boar Bristle

Gift:
Fierceness and speed

Mentor:
Mrs. Renquist,
Madam Swallowtail

FAIRY TEAM

Luna

Madam Swallowtail

NAME:
Hope Valdez

FAIRY NAME AND SPIRIT:
Luna

WAND:
Single Thorn from Prickly
Pear Cactus

GIFT:
Strength, endurance, and
ability to perform magic
without a wand

MENTOR:
Amelia Thompson,
Madam Finch

NAME:
Mrs. Renquist

FAIRY NAME AND SPIRIT:
Madam Swallowtail

WAND:
White Clover Blossom

GIFT:
Strength and endurance

MENTOR TO:
Primrose, Snapdragon,
and Hollyhock

Inside you is the power to do anything™

The Fairy Chronicles

Marigold and the Feather of Hope, the Journey Begins

Dragonfly and the Web of Dreams

Thistle and the Shell of Laughter

Firefly and the Quest of the Black Squirrel

Spiderwort and the Princess of Haiku

Periwinkle and the Cave of Courage

Cinnabar and the Island of Shadows

Mimosa and the River of Wisdom

Primrose and the Magic Snowglobe

Luna and the Well of Secrets

Come visit us at fairychronicles.com

$\mathscr{C}$ontents

Chapter One: The Gargoyle Council 1

Chapter Two: Ripper, the Gremlin 14

Chapter Three: The Banished Dwarf 23

Chapter Four: Primrose 29

Chapter Five: Fairy Circle 39

Chapter Six: Solving the Mystery 58

Chapter Seven: The Magic Snowglobe . . . 71

Chapter Eight: Decisions 83

Fairy Fun 98

Fairy Facts 104

The Gargoyle
Council

The Gargoyle Council had not met for hundreds of years. In fact, Melitus, the leader of the gargoyles, had sat still for so long on top of his cathedral that he had to think for a long while before he could remember how to move. When he finally remembered how to walk, he set off on a three-day journey to the place where the gargoyles were to meet. He traveled mainly at night, so as not to alarm human beings, who might think it odd to see a man of stone wandering around.

Melitus was a gargoyle with a human face and form, rather than an animal. The gargoyles he would be meeting with were all human-form gargoyles, since the animal gargoyles had their own Council.

As far as any gargoyle knew, Melitus was the oldest gargoyle. He was made of pale gray granite, so pale that he was almost white with just a hint of a smoky gray tinge. Melitus was tall and thin, and his long face was etched with deep lines on his forehead and crevices below his cheekbones. Many cracks and chips covered his ancient body. Long ago, he had lost one of his narrow, pointed ears during a renovation to the cathedral. He also had a large chunk of stone missing from his chin.

Melitus grumbled as he walked. This was highly irregular—gargoyles walking around at night. He preferred to do normal gargoyle things like sitting, watching, and waiting.

Of course, these were not the only things gargoyles did. They sometimes warded off evil spirits or other foul creatures seeking to enter churches, cathedrals, and other buildings under the protection of gargoyles. But the gargoyles never had to move to do this because they had their own brand of special gargoyle magic. One look of recognition from a gargoyle was usually enough to send most evil creatures and spirits running. It was never wise to challenge a man of stone and magic.

A sparrow had brought the message to Melitus that Cuthbert, one of Melitus' magistrates, was calling the Gargoyle Council. This was so unexpected that the sparrow had to repeat the message to Melitus five times. Finally, the weary sparrow got his point across to the gargoyle leader, and gladly departed, vowing to carry messages only for the brownies and fairies from now on, because Gargoyle messages were just too much work.

The Gargoyle Council took place at the foot of a granite mountain. Inside a circle of pale white boulders, the gargoyles were gathering. There were many different types of gargoyles. Some were smooth, others rough. And some were fat, while others were thin.

Cuthbert, the gargoyle who had called the Council, was squat, fat, and pale pink in color. His head was round with flabby jowls, big lips, and bulging eyes. He had the appearance of someone whose head was much too large for his body, which was saying something, considering that Cuthbert was probably the largest gargoyle ever seen, widthwise.

Most of the gargoyles were about three to four feet in height, with the exception of Melitus who was almost five feet tall. The assembled gargoyles all sat near the edge of the circle of boulders, waiting anxiously for the meeting to begin.

After Melitus arrived, and determined that all of the gargoyles who needed to be there were present, he called the meeting to order. "Magistrate Cuthbert has called this Council to discuss the issue of Burchard."

With this introduction, the fat pink Cuthbert rose and made his way to the center of the circle, dragging another gargoyle with him by the shoulder.

Burchard was a dark gray granite color and was much leaner than Cuthbert. He had a muscular appearance and a sternly chiseled face. His chin was slightly pointed, as was his nose; and he had sharp, prominent cheekbones. Burchard was one of the few gargoyles that bore the mark of his maker. The sculptor who made Burchard had signed his work. Burchard had a small, heart-shaped leaf with a cross in the center carved into the back of his calf. Burchard did not know who had carved him, and he did not know the meaning of the artist's symbol. The cross was understandable because Burchard had been placed on top of a church, but he didn't know what the leaf might mean. However, Burchard was very proud that the artist had thought enough of his work to leave his mark.

Cuthbert was excited, and breathless, as he addressed the Council. And he spoke very loudly so that one-eared Melitus could hear each word clearly. "I have fired Burchard because of his behavior!"

All around the circle of gargoyles sounds of gasping, wheezing, coughing, and even cracking were heard. Several of the gargoyles had developed fresh cracks

from the shock of Cuthbert's statement. No gargoyle had ever been fired from his job before.

Burchard just stared blankly, as Cuthbert waited for the noises to die down before he went on. "This all started three weeks ago," Cuthbert continued. "From my perch on top of St. Anthony's, I observed Burchard walking along the edges of the roof of his building. He walked for hours. When I questioned him about this, he informed me that he did not know why he did it, but that he just couldn't sit still any longer."

Several of the circled gargoyles were whispering to one another. Melitus took matters in hand. "Quiet now!" he rumbled. "Let us hear the rest of the story."

"Well, I thought that a warning would have been enough to keep him in line," said Cuthbert. "But this week, I caught him up and about again. Not only had he wandered around the roof of his own building, but I also found him walking on the roof of the school next to his church. I am magistrate of gargoyles for that sector of the city. He is my responsibility. His actions reflect on me. I had no choice but to fire him." Cuthbert sounded very pleased with himself as he breathlessly finished.

Melitus waited awhile, thinking, before he spoke. "Very well," he finally said. "Now tell us your side of this, Burchard."

Burchard began speaking calmly. His voice was low and firm, but with a soft edge to it. "I cannot tell you how this happened. I *can* tell you that three weeks ago, I was sitting doing my job, when I felt a sudden urge to stretch my legs. When I stood up, it felt right. When I walked, it was as though I was born to walk. When I sat back down, I felt okay for a few hours. But then I had the urge to rise and walk again. The urge was so strong that I could not sit still. Now,

I am only able to sit still for about two hours at a time. Then I must walk a little before I can sit again."

Many of the gargoyles were looking at Burchard as though he were an alien from another planet. Their eyes fixed on him, and their mouths open, they couldn't believe what they were hearing. None of them had ever had an urge to stand before, much less walk around. It had been a great inconvenience and bother to make the journey to the Gargoyle Council.

Burchard then added, "I believe I can still do my job. In fact, I can get better visibility circling, rather than simply sitting still. I am appealing to you for the chance to prove this. I will maintain my duties, even though I will be mobile."

Melitus stared intently at Burchard for a long time before he spoke. Then he said, "I believe that you probably can carry out the function of protecting your building

Burchard

and its occupants well enough. However, you might be seen. Human beings are not used to seeing gargoyles walk around. If you were ever observed, it would not be acceptable. And I do not think your movements could avoid detection forever. Humans are very intelligent. A few of them might dismiss a moving gargoyle as a figment of their imaginations, but not all of them would."

The other gargoyles in the Council nodded in agreement.

"Having heard both sides," added Melitus, "I am ready to give you my pronouncement." (All of the other gargoyles leaned forward expectantly.) "Burchard, you are only suspended at this time. I am sending you to the fairies. They are problem solvers and fixers. Those are the main functions of fairies, along with protecting nature. Since your behavior is very odd and goes against gargoyle nature, the fairies may be able to help you figure out what has caused this problem and find a way to fix it. We will contact Madam Toad, the leader of the fairies for this region, and explain the circumstances to her. With her approval, you will travel to meet with her."

Burchard agreed, since there wasn't anything else he could do. But Cuthbert mumbled to himself and scowled. He didn't like Melitus overturning his firing of Burchard. It was his opinion that magistrates should not be second-guessed.

Chapter Two

Ripper, the Gremlin

This was the fourth night in a row that Ripper had hidden in the same closet. Ripper lived in Mr. and Mrs. Walker's house, along with four other gremlins. Of course, Mr. and Mrs. Walker had no idea that they had gremlins living with them because gremlins were invisible to regular people. They both just thought that they had rotten luck.

Most of their appliances were broken, including the vacuum cleaner, which was one of the three things that gremlins were afraid of, the other two things being stainless steel and dachshunds. The vacuum cleaner was the first thing Ripper and his friends broke when they moved in nearly six weeks ago. Breaking things was the only ambition gremlins had in life. Their joy and happiness came from destroying machinery, appliances, and mechanical devices of all kinds.

At about a foot high each, and lumpy all over, with grayish-green mottling, gremlins were some of the nastiest of all earth spirits. And they were very frightening because they also had reddish-yellow eyes, long claws, and sharp yellow teeth. Some of the older gremlins had tufts of coarse hair sticking out of their bat-like ears. But Ripper and his friends were juvenile gremlins, without hairy-tufted ears.

Slash, Ripper, Splinter, Cracker, and Basher had traveled together successfully for some time, seeking out new houses as needed for a fresh supply of unbroken equipment and appliances. Since the gang had landed in Mr. and Mrs. Walker's house six weeks ago, it was nearly time to move on.

Now the reason Ripper had been hiding in the closet was to avoid any contact with his friends. For nearly a week, he had felt the strongest urge to fix things, rather than break them. The sensation had become so powerful that he finally gave in four nights ago. He camped out in the closet with a flashlight and some tools, and set to work on fixing a toaster and a set of headphones.

In the last three nights, he had repaired several small appliances including a blow dryer, a hand mixer, two lamps, a cordless phone, an electric razor, and a blender. This was the most fun Ripper ever had. But unfortunately, his fun was about to come to an end.

The door of the closet had opened silently, so Ripper had no idea what was coming until he heard, "*What* are you doing? What on *earth* are you doing? What *are* you doing?" Slash, the leader of their gang, was glaring at him with flashing angry eyes, while the other gremlins just stared, jaws dropped.

There was no use denying anything. There could be no excuses or fancy explanations. They knew. They knew because of the tools. Gremlins didn't need tools to break things. The only reason for tools was to fix things. Ripper had been caught. "I . . . um . . . uh . . ." he sputtered. "Well . . . I . . . guess I just wanted to try to . . . fix something . . . so we could break it again."

The other gremlins were not convinced. And all of them were now grinning evilly at him.

"Nice try," said Cracker.

The rest of the gremlins had started snarling and hissing.

"But . . . I . . . I . . . I guess I don't know what I am doing," admitted Ripper. "A few days ago, I just felt the urge to fix something. When I fixed the toaster, it was kind of fun. So I kept on, with other things. Maybe you should all try this. You might like it."

That was about all that Slash and the others could take. They grabbed Ripper and threw him out into the yard. Circling him, they snapped and slashed at him with their long teeth and claws.

The only thing that saved Ripper was a tool he was carrying. He swung the heavy wrench around in circles and knocked the other gremlins away. Then he started running, as fast as his little legs could carry him. Ripper had sustained two bites and several deep scratches, but he was able to run. Clutching the wrench tightly in one hand, with a screwdriver in

the other, he ran as fast as any gremlin ever had, away from the Walker's yard, and away from the other gremlins. The last thing Ripper heard was Slash yelling sarcastically, "If you like to fix things, go live with the fairies!"

Slash and his buddies immediately left the Walker's house and made their way to Gremlin Junction on the edge of town. Gremlin Junction was basically just an abandoned shack in a field on a run-down soybean farm. Gremlins met there occasionally, haphazardly, to discuss the best homes to try to invade and to warn others of the locations of dachshunds.

As soon as they arrived at the shack, Slash reported Ripper to the Gremlin

Grand Hoohah—an older, extremely vicious gremlin named Crusher. There wasn't any need for discussion like there had been at the Gargoyle Council. Grand Hoohah Crusher immediately gave orders for all other gremlins to find Ripper, and if possible, to destroy him.

Chapter Three

The Banished Dwarf

Well, the unthinkable had happened—unthinkable as far as dwarves were concerned. Not only had Mr. Horatio-dorn-snellick-clang Jones revealed his own secret dwarf name to an outsider (a passing elf), but he had also shared two of his dwarf neighbors' names: one with a witch, and the other with a family of squirrels.

This was unheard of, and unbelievable, because dwarves were masters of keeping secrets. They never shared their names with anyone outside of the dwarf community. The neighbors, Mr. Manbar-van-zip-kobkin

Wright and Mr. Borilla-rus-don-mcfadden Brown, were both extremely angry.

The damage was not extreme though. The witch who had heard Mr. Wright's name dismissed the event and promptly forgot the name. She had never encountered a dwarf who couldn't keep a secret, so she basically thought he was joking. The family of squirrels couldn't speak or write. So even though they believed that they actually *had* heard Mr. Brown's name, they couldn't share it with anyone. And the elf privy to Mr. Jones' name was none other than Staid, the protector of the Shell of Laughter. He was far too busy spreading laughter around the world to converse with very many other creatures, so it was highly unlikely that the name would be spread by elf means.

However, the problem was growing because it hadn't stopped with the names. Only the day before, Dwarf Jones had given away a trade secret for polishing copper to a passing pie salesman. Dwarves were master craftsmen of metal and stone, and they guarded their workmanship techniques with their best secret-keeping capacities.

So this had been the last straw for the neighbors and the entire dwarf community. The dwarves had called a Regional Dwarf Assembly to discuss the offenses and possible punishment.

The Head Dwarf's voice boomed as he spoke to his listeners. "Secrets are a dwarf trademark, an institution! To reveal them is unheard of! This is a crime that must be punished!"

Dwarf Jones was given a chance to explain himself, but his explanation sounded lame, even to his own ears. "I don't know why I did it. I just felt that I needed to. It's like I had kept things in too long, and they had to come out. I apologize to Dwarf Wright and Dwarf

Brown, but I just couldn't stop myself. I started talking, and the names just came out.

"And the pie salesman was very friendly," Dwarf Jones added. "He was telling me how he crafts his own pie tins. We got to talking further, and drinking espresso, and he told me about his favorite copper cooking pot. He uses it to cook pie filling, and he said he could never seem to get it polished up good. It seemed neighborly to share our copper polishing technique with him. I know I shouldn't have, but I couldn't stop myself."

The Head Dwarf thought for a few minutes, then addressed the assembly again. "That doesn't explain *why* this has happened. No dwarf has ever revealed secrets before without the best of reasons, and usually only in emergencies." Then, speaking to Dwarf Jones directly, he added, "Perhaps you have some sort of disease. I don't want any other dwarves catching what you have, or getting the idea that your behavior is acceptable in any way." Next, louder, and with much authority, the Head Dwarf announced, "Horatio-dorn-snellick-clang Jones, you are banished into exile until you can provide a more in-depth reason why you revealed dwarf secrets, and until you can promise everyone here never to breach our confidences again!"

The finality in this statement didn't allow room for any more discussion. And looking around the assembly, Mr. Jones could see that he had very little support. He went home quickly and stuffed a few things into a small knapsack. Then he set out right away. He knew exactly where he was going and who to ask for help.

Chapter Four

Primrose

So far, Christmas break had been uneventful. Taylor Buchanan had kept busy finishing presents she was making for family and friends, helping her mom with cooking and baking, and reading a new mystery novel. Taylor loved mysteries. They were her favorites of all books. And she often had them figured out well before the end. It was usually the button on the floor or the toothpick in the ashtray that gave the criminal away. Taylor was always able to pick up on these small clues faster than the detectives in the stories.

Taylor was looking forward to two exciting things this Christmas vacation. One was her birthday on Christmas Eve, when she would turn ten years old, and the other was a very special gathering of friends that she would be attending tomorrow, Saturday.

In addition to being just like other girls her age, Taylor was also a fairy. She had been given the fairy spirit of a pink flower known as evening primrose that grew wild in meadows and on roadsides in Texas and other Southern states.

Standard fairy form was six inches. When fairies were in fairy form, regular people could not recognize them. Non-magical people would only be able to see the fairy spirits such as flowers, bats, dragonflies, berries, tiny reptiles, herbs, tree blossoms, moths, small animals, and such like.

As a fairy, Primrose had tiny gold wings and wore a dress made of pale pink,

translucent flower petals with delicate gold veins. The dress came to just above her knees, and she wore soft pink slippers and a crown of primrose blossoms to match. She also had shoulder length, wavy blond hair and lots of freckles.

The Saturday gathering Primrose was looking forward to was called Fairy Circle. The fairies in this region met regularly for celebration, and to solve serious problems. This year alone, many of Primrose's fairy friends had gone on five daring missions that had saved all of mankind from death, chaos, torment, misery, and widespread ignorance. Primrose herself had never been directly involved in any of these missions; but she hoped one day to be selected to go on a fairy adventure, to make her own important contribution to the fairies' work.

In addition to being able to fly and perform magic, each fairy was given a unique fairy gift, which was sort of like a strength or specialty. Fairy gifts were usually what prompted Madam Toad to select certain fairies for particular missions.

Primrose's strength was her attention to detail and her ability to solve mysteries by picking up on the smallest of details. She could connect the un-connectable to figure out how things had happened and what they would lead to. She was so observant and shrewd that nothing could be hidden from her. Also, because evening primroses usually opened at night, which was how the flower got its name, Primrose was given the gift of extra energy after dark.

Being somewhat of a bookworm, and in the category of the "thinker" fairies, Primrose doubted that she would ever be chosen to lead a fairy mission. But she very much longed to be included in one. She felt she could really make a difference if given a chance. But she also trusted Madam Toad's judgment. Under Madam

Toad's strong leadership and direction, the fairies of the Southwest region had never failed on a mission.

Primrose's cousin, Justine Macintyre, was deaf. She had lost her hearing as a baby when she was very ill and ran a high fever. Primrose and Justine were the same age, and Justine was also blessed with a fairy spirit—that of a blue hollyhock flower.

By the time Primrose and Hollyhock were five years old, Primrose was fluent in American Sign Language. She had always been able to communicate well with her cousin and could now interpret for her, so Hollyhock was able interact more easily with others. However, Hollyhock could also read lips very well, so she didn't always need Primrose's help. Being observant and able to pick up on details were the reasons it had been so easy for Primrose to learn sign language at such a young age.

Fairy activities were usually limited this time of year, especially for fairies with flower fairy spirits. Very few flowers bloomed at Christmastime, and it could be dangerous for fairies if people observed flowers blooming out of season, especially because some flower enthusiasts liked to pick flowers and smash them into books and presses.

Younger fairies limited their fairy activities anyway unless their mentors were present. In fact, no young fairy was allowed to perform fairy magic without approval from a fairy mentor. And no fairy of any age could use fairy powers for trivial matters, to abuse others, or to solve personal problems. These things were simply not allowed. Fairies had an important job to do, and they had to strictly follow the Fairy Code of Conduct.

Madam Swallowtail was mentor for both Primrose and Hollyhock. She also

mentored a slightly younger fairy named Snapdragon. Madam Swallowtail's real name was Mrs. Renquist. She was one of the sponsors for the local chapter of Girls Club. This was an ideal situation for her to be in so that she could identify young fairies and provide excuses for the girls to spend time away from home while engaging in fairy activities. In fairy form, Madam Swallowtail wore a black dress with a bluish sheen; and she had large black wings with glowing ivory eyespots.

Fairy wands could be made from almost anything and were enchanted to help fairies perform their magic. Primrose's wand was a small black raven feather. Hollyhock had a polished splinter of silver birch. And Madam Swallowtail carried a white clover blossom wand that looked like a tiny fireworks explosion.

The fairies each carried a pouch of pixie dust and the fairy handbook on their belts. Pixie dust was used in many capacities during fairy magic making, and the handbook was an interactive source of fairy information. The book contained answers to fairy questions and advice to help fairies make wise decisions.

A nut message from Madam Swallowtail had informed Primrose of the pick-up time for Fairy Circle the next day. Primrose went to bed early, trying to get to sleep quickly. Sleep was the fastest way to the next day, and she was looking forward to seeing Madam Swallowtail, Hollyhock, and all of her other fairy friends.

Chapter Five

Fairy Circle

Ripper was hiding again, but not from gremlins this time. He was in Madam Toad's side yard, carefully crouching behind the steps of her gazebo. In the back of his mind were the last words he had heard from Slash: "*If you like to fix things, go live with the fairies!*"

Well, Ripper didn't want to live with fairies. Fairies and gremlins did not get along with each other, so living together would be out of the question. But he did want to ask Madam Toad for help.

Ripper spotted Madam Toad early in the morning when she came outside wearing her bathrobe to pick up the early edition of the newspaper from her driveway.

Madam Toad was actually Mrs. Jenkins when she was in woman form, as she was this morning. She would not take on fairy form until she got to Fairy Circle. Mrs. Jenkins, however, unlike regular human beings, could see gremlins since she was also a fairy. She saw the slight movement by the gazebo steps and peered closely at the spot, immediately recognizing the tips of the ears and clawed fingers just visible beside the third step. "Hello there!" she called.

Gremlins were usually very mean and nasty spirits, and because of their sharp teeth and claws, they could be dangerous to fairies. Gremlins and fairies also had direct opposite purposes in life—breaking versus fixing. For this reason, gremlins and fairies avoided each other whenever possible.

But Madam Toad had very little to fear from any other magical creature. She was one of the most powerful fairies that had ever lived, and she could face off with a hundred gremlins, if needed, without serious problem. Most of the gremlins in the area knew this, and no gremlin had ever set foot inside her yard before.

Madam Toad was indeed curious about this one, so she called to him again. "I give you my word as leader of the fairies that I will do you no harm. Please, come out from behind the steps and talk to me."

So Ripper did.

Madam Swallowtail picked up her three young charges very early, before eight o'clock. It was a long drive to the secluded bit of woods where the fairies would be meeting. She had arranged with all of their parents for the three of them to go to a Girls Club activity and to have a sleepover at her home afterward, so the girls could attend Fairy Circle and possibly go on an adventure if chosen by Madam Toad.

Snapdragon's real name was Bettina Gregory. As a fairy, she wore a dress made of fluffy, orange and yellow, furled snapdragon petals. She had short, curly, light brown hair; and her wand was a black boar bristle that was spiraled like a corkscrew. Her special fairy gift was a fierce ability to defend, protect, and even attack, if necessary. The snapdragon flower got its name from the center of the flower's resemblance to the mouth of a dragon. The gift of fierceness came from this. Snapdragon was also very swift when flying, just like a speedy dragon.

As they arrived at the Fairy Circle, Madam Swallowtail told the girls, "We are meeting under a blackthorn tree today.

The blackthorn is symbolic of change and represents new beginnings." The fairies were always interested in learning about the types of trees they met under because the trees usually had special significance to the purpose of their gathering.

The blackthorn tree was more like a large, thorny shrub. This time of year, it didn't have leaves, or its white flowers, but the tree did have fruit that looked like small purple plums. The lower branches of the blackthorn had been decorated with bewitched cranberries that were glowing like beautiful red lanterns.

In the middle of the Fairy Circle, a fire crackled merrily in a fairy fire shield. The fire shield was a shallow iron bowl used to protect the earth from scarring by fairy campfires.

Several fairies were already at the meeting by the time Primrose and the others arrived. But as they approached the gathering, Primrose, Snapdragon, Hollyhock, and even Madam Swallowtail stopped dead in their tracks. They had had many visitors to Fairy Circle before including elves, leprechauns, brownies, dwarves, trolls, and even Mother Nature herself, but today's visitors were certainly most unusual.

The dwarf was not very unusual, but none of the fairies had ever seen a moving gargoyle before. And the fairies who had seen gremlins knew to stay well away from them. It was usually the job of dachshunds and vacuum cleaners to deal with gremlins, not fairies. They approached cautiously. The gremlin was sitting close to Madam Toad and looked almost afraid to stray too far from her.

The dwarf was just over three feet tall and was dressed in loose, gray and white clothing that was typical of dwarf miners and craftsmen. His head nearly touched the lower limbs of the blackthorn tree while he visited with Dragonfly and Rosemary who were hovering near his shoulder.

The gargoyle wasn't visiting with anyone at present. He was walking in circles around the edges of the gathering, as though guarding the fairies. The expression on his face was very stern and watchful as he contemplated his protection duties. He took this job very seriously, just as he had his old job, though it would be very unlikely for an evil spirit to approach a gathering of fairies. Fairies in great numbers were an awesome power. Very few creatures could harm a group of fairies because their individual gifts could combine to form an extremely strong and diverse protective force.

A few of the fairies looked up gargoyles in their handbooks since they had never met one. This is the information that the fairy handbook shared:

Gargoyles: Most gargoyles are made of stone. They are carved and sculpted, then placed on build-ings—most commonly religious buildings. Gargoyles are mythically believed to have the ability to ward off evil spirits to protect a building and its occupants. However, the original architectural use of gargoyles was as waterspouts, extending from gutters, to channel rainwater and melting snow runoff. Gargoyles can be carved to resemble either humans or animals, or a combination of both. Many gargoyles are magical, under the guardianship of Mother Nature, and do indeed serve to protect.

As more fairies arrived, all of them were surprised to see their interesting visitors. Madam Toad encouraged Ripper and Burchard to circulate and introduce themselves, which they did, reluctantly. Luna, one of the moth fairies, was very interested in getting to know Burchard. She loved reading stories about gargoyles.

Luna's real name was Hope Valdez. She had pale green wings with very large eyespots. Her luminous wings also had soft pink edges and a long curving tail. Luna's dress and slippers were a light, misty green color; and she had straight dark hair that fell to just below her shoulders. Madam Finch was her mentor.

The other fairies loved talking to Luna. She was so interesting because when she was younger she had lived in Mexico with her grandparents. She spoke both Spanish and English, and she often told the other girls stories about the colorful customs and traditions of the people of Mexico. Luna and her parents often traveled back to Mexico to visit family and attend some of the festivals and celebrations that were part of their heritage.

Luna was also one of the most unique fairies that ever existed. She carried a wand made of a single thorn from a prickly pear cactus. The thorn was long, gleaming white, and sharp like a needle. But she never used it and never needed to because Luna was the only fairy who could perform fairy magic without a wand.

Madam Toad and Madam Finch had discussed this issue thoroughly when it was discovered that Luna could perform wand magic with a simple flick of her finger or wave of her hand, and sometimes with just a look or a glance. None of the older fairies had ever heard of a fairy being able to do this. They decided that Luna was likely one of the most powerful fairies ever created, and that her ability to perform magic without a wand was probably an extra fairy gift. Luna had been given extraordinary eyesight as another of her fairy gifts. And like all butterfly and moth fairies, she also had great strength and endurance.

On the other side of Fairy Circle, Dewberry, Spiderwort, Lily, Thistle, Firefly, and Madam June Beetle were visiting with the dwarf, who was now sitting cross-legged, thoroughly enjoying himself being surrounded by beautiful fairies. As the dwarf told them his name, the fairies' mouths all dropped open, and they stared at him in shock. "But you can call me Mr. Jones," he added, "since my first name is so long and hard to remember."

Marigold, Morning Glory, Skipper, Cisthene, Madam Mum, and Madam Chameleon all edged up to the gremlin to say hello. After all, there was safety in numbers. He quietly talked to them about the last few houses he had occupied and about the run of unusually warm weather. Ripper also proudly shared which particular things he was especially good at breaking. (Coffee makers, refrigerators, and lawn mowers were his specialties.)

As they talked, Madam Mum started fiddling with her watch, which had stopped. She asked Madam Chameleon, "Do you have the time, Kathy? My watch has been acting up for about a week."

"I might be able to help you with that," said Ripper, pulling a tiny jeweler's tool out of a zippered pocket in the wide belt he was wearing.

This group of fairies was just as shocked as those gathered around the dwarf. No one had ever heard of gremlin that could fix anything, or wanted to.

Madam Mum silently handed her watch to Ripper who expertly popped off the back. Then he poked and prodded the watch innards for a few moments. Next, he snapped the pieces back together and deftly wound and set the watch, handing it back to the still speechless Madam Mum. He grinned at the fairies sheepishly, and they all burst out in applause. They were impressed not only with Ripper's ability to fix the watch; but also, the tool he had used was made of stainless steel, something gremlins usually avoided at all costs. This was certainly unexpected.

Burchard had been talking politely and stoically to Madam Rose, Snapdragon, and Moonflower. However, he was unable to stand still for long and soon excused himself to again walk around the perimeter of the gathering. Silently circling the tree, he watched them all carefully, keeping a lookout for anything evil that might approach.

Next, the fairies and their guests all had refreshments. This was the special Christmas Fairy Circle. So in addition to enjoying their usual treats of homemade fudge, raspberries, powdered sugar puff pastries, lemon jellybeans, and peanut butter and marshmallow crème sandwiches, they also had cranberry relish on

crackers, gingerbread cookies, snicker-doodles, tiny pecan pies, candy cane crunch cookies, cherry chip loaf, and hot apple cider.

Also, their troll friends had sent some yummy pumpkin cookies. And Madam Toad released an enormous box of her extra-special fairy snowflake divinity. The candy was fluffy, sweet, and creamy just like regular divinity, but it was made into snowflake shapes and was enchanted to hover and swirl about the gathering. Many of the young fairies made a game of flying-chase to catch the swooping, sailing candies. Ripper was especially good at catching the snowflakes and made presentations of many of his captures to the fairies, who were now all thoroughly charmed by the friendly gremlin.

Ripper had also lived in a house for several months where the occupants used sign language, so he was able to visit with

Hollyhock. It was somewhat funny to see a gremlin using sign language. But he was actually very good. Ripper and Hollyhock were able to carry on a long conversation without any help from Primrose or Madam Swallowtail.

On the other side of the Fairy Circle, Madam Chameleon was changing colors, imitating her surroundings, to entertain Pumpkinwing and Teasel. The girls were still giggling and clapping their hands when the meeting was called to order.

Chapter Six

Solving the Mystery

Madam Toad's voice was very loud and festive as she addressed them. "Welcome, everyone! Happy Christmas, Hanukkah, and Kwanzaa!"

When Madam Toad had everyone's attention, she spoke more solemnly. "By now, many of you may have guessed why our visitors are here. It is unusual for a gargoyle to move around, for a gremlin to enjoy fixing things, and for a dwarf to reveal secrets. As far as anyone can tell, these are recent and singular occurrences among gargoyles, gremlins, and dwarves. Burchard has been fired from his job. Ripper has been driven out and is being pursued by other gremlins. And Mr. Jones has been banished by the dwarves.

"We have no idea how or why these things occurred," Madam Toad continued, "and a reason why must be found so that things can be put to right."

Luna raised her hand to ask a question and give input. "What is so wrong with what they have done? It doesn't seem like anyone has been truly hurt by their actions. Maybe the dwarves, gargoyles, and gremlins just need to learn to be more accepting of others. Differences are good. No two fairies are the same, and that is what makes us strong as a group."

"True, true," said Madam Toad. "Everything you have said makes sense. But it seems that these actions were involuntary, and the results have been devastating for the three creatures involved.

"There is no magic that anyone can think of to reverse what has happened. And the dwarf, gremlin, and gargoyle are still having the same urges that got them into trouble with their fellow beings. Even if it can never be changed, this does warrant explanation. We should try to help them figure out how this happened."

The fairies all nodded in understanding as Madam Toad went on. "I have consulted elves, witches, brownies, dwarves, and leprechauns. None of their brands of magic contain any spells or potions that can work for this. It is possible that a regular doctor or therapist could help, with some type of counseling or behavior modification. But we cannot send magical creatures to non-magical people for help. For one thing, the people would not be able to see the gremlin; and they likely wouldn't take the gargoyle or dwarf seriously. It would be too risky to try to find just the right human beings to ask for help.

"I am setting the task of figuring out what has happened, and trying to help sort it out, to Primrose. Snapdragon and Luna will assist, and Madam Swallowtail will supervise.

"That is all," said Madam Toad, and she finished with her familiar parting words. "Now flitter forth fairies and take care of business!"

As they packed up the leftover refreshments, the other fairies all bid the assigned fairy group farewell and wished them luck.

Primrose immediately sat down and pulled out a small notebook and pencil from her belt. Luna, Snapdragon, Madam Swallowtail, Ripper, Burchard, and Mr. Jones all sat with her, quietly and respectfully, waiting for her to begin.

Primrose was truly a pro at this. Even though this was her first mission, she wasn't nervous at all. She was in "detective mode" at once and expertly began asking each of the guests in turn a series of questions, jotting down notes once in awhile as they answered her.

"When did you first feel the urge to move around?

". . . to fix things?

". . . to tell a secret?

"Where have you been in the last three weeks?

"What have you been eating in the last three weeks?

"Have you had any visitors?

"Have you seen anything unusual?

"Did you speak to anyone about the urges—before, during, or after?"

And finally, Primrose asked, "Tell me the exact events that happened on the day you felt the very first urge."

After thinking for a few moments, Burchard told Primrose, "I was just sitting

and watching a pigeon walk by. I remembered thinking that it must be nice to be able to walk, and I wished that I could know what it felt like. I thought about this for a while as I watched a little girl playing in the courtyard below.

"I forgot what I was thinking about when I saw a man staring up at me. He was very tall and had dark hair. I was startled because of the way he was looking at me. It was as though he knew I was not just a piece of stone. I thought he could sense my magic somehow."

Primrose scribbled notes on her pad as Burchard went on telling his story. "The man was carrying a snowglobe, which was not odd for this time of year. He put the snowglobe into his pocket and walked away. But he made me very uneasy, as though he knew exactly what I was, what my job was, and possibly even my name. I knew he wasn't evil. I would have been able to sense that. A few minutes later, I felt the irresistible urge to get up and move around. So I did."

Ripper told his story next. "I was sitting on the porch with Cracker. We had just demolished a dishwasher, and were feeling pretty good about ourselves, when we noticed a man with red hair ride by on a unicycle. We were talking about how fun it would be to mess up the unicycle, when one of the wheel-spokes broke, on its own. No gremlin can break things by thought so we were really confused. The man lost his balance, and for some strange reason, I felt sorry for him.

"He dropped a snowglobe he was carrying and was frantic that it might have broken. But the globe was fine when he picked it up. I remember thinking that it might be fun to fix his spoke for him, and I was wishing that I could help him because he seemed so distraught.

"Then I remembered I was a gremlin and wasn't supposed to fix things," Ripper added sheepishly, "so I didn't think about helping him anymore. But the next morning I started eyeing the toaster and the tools. It was terrible. I couldn't stop myself. It's like I caught a fever, and I couldn't get cured."

Finally, Mr. Jones shared what he was able to remember. "It was about a week before the pie salesman came through. I was working on some iron hinges, and a man stopped by asking for directions to the nearest town with a hospital. I thought he might be injured, but he looked okay, so I didn't offer any help—I just gave him the directions. But I had to tell him a super-long route because I am not allowed to reveal any of the dwarves' secret shortcuts. I remember thinking that it was a shame I couldn't give him instructions for a shorter route, and I wished I could share the secret because most people only travel to a hospital for a good reason, and they usually need to get there quickly. The man was carrying a small snowglobe, which I assumed was a present for someone."

When Mr. Jones finished speaking, Primrose quickly referred to her notes. Almost immediately, she said, "Well, you have all seen a stranger with a snowglobe, and you have all made a wish."

Mr. Jones was shaking his head. "But the strangers didn't look anything alike. Burchard's had dark hair. Ripper's had red hair. And my stranger didn't have any hair at all—he was bald."

"But there is still the connection of the wish and the snowglobe," said Primrose, as she pulled her fairy handbook from her

the **Wishmaker**
is a magical spirit
with the ability
to grant wishes.
......
He can take any
form, and travels
around granting
wishes with the
help of his
Magic Snow-
globe.

belt and began flipping the pages. She looked up wishes first and read the entry aloud to her friends:

"*Wishes*: *Wishes are closely related to hopes, desires, and dreams. People make wishes for many reasons, but mainly in an attempt to gain something greatly desired— either physical, emotional, or spiritual. A magical being called the Wishmaker has the ability to grant wishes.*"

Primrose next looked up Wishmaker:

"*Wishmaker*: *The Wishmaker is a magical spirit with the ability to grant wishes. He can take any form, and travels around granting wishes with the help of his Magic Snowglobe. The Wishmaker*

is often found near hospitals,
granting wishes to children who
are sick or family members of those
who are ill."

"This is the answer!" said Primrose excitedly. "He can take any form he likes; that is why he looked different to each of you. We need to seek him out right away to ask him to help you. There is only one hospital in the city," she added. "Since Ripper and Mr. Jones both live near here, and saw the Wishmaker recently, I am hopeful he is still in the area and hasn't moved on yet."

Chapter Seven

The Magic
Snowglobe

The fairies, gargoyle, gremlin, and dwarf set out immediately. Since Burchard and Mr. Jones were both fairly large, they kept to the shadows to avoid being seen. Both Primrose and Snapdragon were also careful not to be seen, since the flowers would have looked unusual blooming out of season.

They hadn't traveled very far when a commotion was heard behind them: loud sounds of things being knocked over, and noisy crashing about. Several gremlins had spotted Ripper and were pursuing him.

They were snarling, spitting, and being very ugly as they drew closer.

The fairies were very frightened, all except Snapdragon. She wasn't having any of this nonsense on her first fairy mission. Right away, she took action. She raised her boar bristle wand and sent orange sparks flying at the gremlins.

At first, this didn't bother them; but Snapdragon became more determined as the gremlins came closer. She swooped about their heads, and the sparks from her wand turned into tiny fireballs that scorched the gremlins' ears and noses.

Ripper remembered his last encounter with his fellow gremlins and was afraid. As the gremlins lunged at him, Burchard stepped in to help. Gremlins would never be able to hurt a stone man. He kicked two of them, knocking them backwards several feet. Then, he picked up another three and tossed them into a cold dark alley.

The gremlins soon decided they had had enough of being scorched, booted, and tossed; and they scurried away from Snapdragon and Burchard.

"Don't worry," Burchard said solemnly to Ripper. "As long as I am with you, no one will harm you. I promise."

Ripper smiled. He was happy to have such a powerful friend.

Three blocks from the hospital, the fairies took to walking, instead of flying, so there would be less chance of getting

noticed, especially since they were nearing a place with a lot more people milling about.

As they stopped for a moment on the edge of a vacant lot, Primrose gave a loud cry of pain. A fire ant had climbed onto her foot and had bitten her ankle. Fire ant bites were horrible and painful to regular-sized people. To a tiny fairy, the burning sting was almost unbearable. The recent, unseasonably warm weather and heavy rains had caused the fire ants to be more active than normal for December. Primrose sat down, unable to stand on her swollen ankle.

Snapdragon used her wand again to drive away a whole swarm of fire ants that were now trying to attack them.

Luna quickly bent down to Primrose. Placing her hand over the bite, she softly uttered the words, *"Heal. Cool."* A thin blue light appeared near her elbow and traveled down her forearm to her hand to cover the swollen bite.

Relief was instantaneous. Within a second, Primrose's ankle was no longer swollen, and there wasn't even a red mark of any kind from the bite. "Wow! Thank you!" she said to Luna. Then she asked, "You have healing powers too?"

"No," answered Luna. "It's a regular *Healing Spell.* I just don't need a wand to do it." The other fairies were very impressed.

"I hate fire ants!" said Primrose, angrily. "I wish we could just zap all of them out of existence."

"Be careful what you wish for, Primrose," said Madam Swallowtail quickly. "They must serve some purpose, or they wouldn't exist."

"But fire ants aren't even supposed to be here," countered Primrose. "They are an introduced pest. They're not indigenous. And it is believed that fire ants are responsible for the decline in the numbers of horned toads and armadillos, because they just can't defend themselves against the ruthless ants."

"That is likely all true," answered Madam Swallowtail. "I am just suggesting that you be careful of what you are wishing for. The Wishmaker is probably very nearby, and he might decide to grant your request. I don't think you really want all fire ants everywhere 'zapped out of existence.' They must be part of a natural balance somewhere."

Primrose nodded reluctantly, agreeing with this wisdom. But it was hard to forget the pain of the bite, and it was hard not to feel sorry for horned toads and armadillos.

It was getting dark when they finally reached the hospital, so the group was less conspicuous. However, Primrose did light the tip of her wand with a little whisper of, *"Fairy light."* She did this more for comfort than anything. None of the younger fairies were usually out much at night.

The group hid behind several trees in a small park next to the hospital and waited, watching the entrances and the people going in and out.

"Just keep an eye out for a snowglobe," said Primrose, "since he can look like anyone."

After only a few moments of watching, Luna smiled, knowingly. She didn't just have powerful eyesight. Her sight-gift allowed her to see things as they really were, to look past appearances that were often deceptive. She told the others, "I think that man over there might be the Wishmaker." She was pointing to an old man sitting on a bench near the main hospital entrance.

"It's too risky to approach him now," said Primrose. "Too many people are going in and out of the hospital. We will have to wait until later."

Wishmaker

But they didn't have to wait long to meet the Wishmaker. After about ten minutes, the old man rose from the bench and wandered over to the park. He was dressed very shabbily, in tattered clothes with many patches. His coat had worn-out elbows, and the scarf around his neck was ripped and ragged. He also stooped and looked like a homeless man, very down on his luck, with long, matted hair and a messy, bushy beard.

The old man slipped quietly between the trees to stand very near the gargoyle and dwarf, who were kneeling in the shrubs. None of the members of the party were visible to him. They were all expertly hiding.

When he was completely out of sight of the hospital comers and goers, the shabby man transformed into a beautiful being of light. The Wishmaker was a milky white color all over and was dressed in long, flowing robes. Since the glow from his aura was very bright, he slipped a little farther back into the foliage to avoid any detection.

"I believe you are looking for me," the spirit said quietly to the trees and shrubs. Then he patiently waited for the fairies, dwarf, gremlin, and gargoyle to reveal themselves.

As they made their way into his presence, the Wishmaker slipped his Magic Snowglobe out of the pocket of his robes. It was about the size of a small grapefruit, and was perfectly round, with no base or stand attached to it. The brilliant, shining globe was filled with sparkling white snow, falling and swirling gently. There was no winter scene inside the glass sphere, just snow, but its simple beauty mesmerized all the members of the group.

Decisions

s there something you would like to discuss with me?" the Wishmaker asked softly.

Ripper spoke first. "I think you are the cause of my problems. I can't stop myself from wanting to fix things, and I never feel like breaking things anymore. The other gremlins are after me. They will kill me if they can. The only reason I am alive now is because of the protection of Burchard and Snapdragon."

Mr. Jones addressed the Wishmaker next. "Since I met you and gave you directions, I can't seem to stop telling secrets. I have been banished from the dwarf community for this."

And finally, Burchard told the Wishmaker, "I have lost my job because I want to be active and can no longer sit still without getting up to stretch my legs occasionally. I want to return to work, and I am unhappy that I cannot."

The Wishmaker gazed thoughtfully at the gremlin, dwarf, and gargoyle for a few moments before he spoke. "I *can* undo the wishes I granted you," he finally told them. "However, I want to share something with you first, and I want you to think carefully about what I tell you before you make any final decisions.

"I can only grant wishes that are truly desired. The wishes I granted you involve your characters, personalities, and inner selves. I can never grant these types of wishes unless there is something there to work with, a starting point, if you will. There was already something deep inside each of you that was a part of you to begin with that made you make the wishes in the first place.

"Let me give you an example," the Wishmaker added. "I can never make someone fall in love with another person if they don't really want to. When I grant wishes for love, there is always at least a little love already in place, underlying, like a spark.

"At some level, I think you have all been upset at one time or another with the things you were doing—breaking things, keeping secrets, and never moving around. I believe you all wanted to change, to become something different, even if it was against what was expected of you." The Wishmaker paused briefly, then spoke again, very softly. "Life is ever changing. It cannot stay stagnant. We all grow, mature, develop, and change. That is how we make our contributions to this world, and how the world often changes for the better.

"I will give you some time to think about what I have said. Then, if you want me to un-grant the wishes, I will. But I can offer you a solution, if any of you decide to keep the wishes I granted you. It is a safe haven: a place where you can all live, and work, and be yourselves. I will return in one hour to hear your decisions." With this, the Wishmaker changed back into the old man and made his way once again to the bench near the hospital entrance.

Burchard, Ripper, and Mr. Jones sat quietly together for some time, thinking things over. The fairies stayed off to one side and did not interfere, since it was a big decision for each of the three to make.

Ripper told his companions, "I like fixing things. I'm not sure I want to go back to breaking things. If the Wishmaker knows of a place where I can be safe and fix things, I think I will keep the wish he granted me."

Burchard was nodding, as he said, "I don't like the idea of returning to an entirely motionless existence. I know I can do a good job of protecting as a mobile gargoyle. If I can still work as a protector, I would like to keep my wish as well."

And finally, Mr. Jones gave his input. "I have been struggling for years with keeping secrets that don't seem to make any sense. It doesn't hurt to help people find a shortcut. Plus, I think it is good to share a bit of dwarf knowledge of crafting techniques to make the world a better place. I would like to teach some of these things to others. And I have always felt silly not being able to share my name.

"I like telling people useful things," he added, "and I like being called by my name. And it is certainly a more interesting life to be able to interact freely with others, outside of the dwarf community. I am determined to keep my wish too, and hope for acceptance somewhere."

The fairies all smiled, happy about the decisions of Mr. Jones, Burchard, and Ripper.

Primrose slipped out from behind a tree to see if she could spot the Wishmaker. Unfortunately, at that moment, two people saw her, a man and woman, who had made their way into the park from the hospital for some fresh air.

"Look, dear!" said the woman. "A primrose flower blooming in winter. There is a legend that if you find a spring flower blooming in winter you get to make a wish, and the wish will come true."

The man didn't say anything, but he smiled and put his arm around the woman's shoulders. They both closed their

eyes and were silent. Primrose didn't move, and neither the man nor the woman made any attempt to touch her. After they had made their wish, they simply turned and walked back to the hospital.

The Wishmaker suddenly appeared behind them in the trees. "They will get their wish," he said kindly. "It was a selfless wish—to heal a loved one."

Then he added, "I can never grant wishes that are extremely selfish. Theirs was a good wish and will bring happiness to many. I will also grant it because they need to continue to have faith and to believe. Even though little primroses can't grant wishes, I can. And there is no harm in letting them think that a wish on a flower can come true."

Then the Wishmaker turned to Burchard, Mr. Jones, and Ripper. "What have you decided?" he asked.

The three were all smiling, as they stood together and announced in unison, "Keep the wishes!"

The Wishmaker was pleased with their choices.

True to his word, the Wishmaker put Burchard, Mr. Jones, and Ripper in touch with a farmer named Mr. Hobson in Missouri. Mr. Hobson and his wife were long-time believers in all things magical, and gladly welcomed the three friends. There were many other magical creatures already living on the farm including gnomes, brownies, trolls, and an ogre. The gnomes did their usual job of growing things and adding colors to nature. The trolls helped with nighttime work. The ogre was in charge of all heavy lifting. And the brownies did small odd jobs, when they weren't busy causing mischief.

Ripper was given the job of supervising repairs to all of the farm and household equipment. He had broken mechanical devices for so long that it was a breeze for him to master reverse-breaking.

Mr. Jones was in charge of news-spreading activities throughout the local farming community. He passed messages back and forth between various farm owners and workers about things such as how many lambs were born, when the potato harvest would begin, and the number of jars of

apple butter put up in each kitchen. There really wasn't any need to keep secrets, so he was happy. He also taught some of his metal-working techniques to the local farmers. They were very appreciative of his crafts-manship and knowledge.

Burchard was in charge of helping Flocksie, the Hobsons' border collie. Together, they guarded and protected the farm and its occupants from coyotes, wild boars, trespassers, and occasionally, evil spirits. Burchard loved his job and was often seen walking the perimeter fences with Flocksie, keeping an eye on things.

Christmas Eve was some- what hectic at the Buchanan household because the family was celebrating Taylor's birthday. Her cousin, Jus- tine, had been over in the afternoon, along with several other friends including Beth, Jensen, Bailey, Vinca, Jennifer, Lenox, Bettina, and Hope. The girls had a lot of fun playing games, and secretly congratulating Primrose on leading her first successful fairy adventure. Then they all enjoyed chocolate cake with strawberry ice cream.

Christmas Day was clear and cool. Taylor and her parents opened gifts before having breakfast together and attending church. Inside a tiny square box addressed to Taylor was the most beautiful miniature snowglobe ever seen. It was about the size of a cherry tomato, and was bright and glowing. A flurry of snow was billowing around in it before the globe was even shaken. There was no card or message to indicate who had sent the gift, but Taylor knew it was from the Wishmaker—a tiny replica of his own Magic Snowglobe.

Mrs. Buchanan was very interested in the gift. "It's so beautiful," she said. "I wonder who gave it to you." Examining the tiny sphere closely, she added, "It doesn't have a scene in it like most snowglobes, just snow. That's odd."

"Probably one of my friends from yesterday put it under the tree, as a secret and surprise gift," answered Taylor. "I like the scene as it is, simple and pure."

Outside her church later that morning, when no one was looking, Taylor made sure to wave at a gargoyle perched on the roof of the main building. Even from a distance, she could see the gargoyle's large, bird-shaped head clearly. And she thought she saw one of his eyes wink at her. She smiled, silently thanking him for the good job he was doing, protecting everyone in the church by warding off evil spirits. She vowed to send him a nut message later, from her fairy self, to say hello and to thank him in writing.

Before she went to bed that night, Taylor made a wish on her tiny snowglobe. She wished for acceptance of each other's differences for all people worldwide. Then

she made a second wish: for the ability of mankind to embrace changes and gain strength from them.

The Wishmaker granted her wishes, to all people in the world whose hearts and minds already included the tiniest ability to understand and accept these things. And the world became a better place.

The End

Fairy Fun

Make a Wish

Although the Wishmaker granted all of the wishes for Primrose and her friends, many people still make wishes on things in hopes that their wish will come true. For example, the man and woman wished on the primrose flower even though primrose flowers cannot grant wishes. Even if it is not necessarily true, it is still fun to wish on things, and maybe the Wishmaker will hear you.

Wishing on birthday candles is always a popular way to make a wish, but here are a few more that you can try:

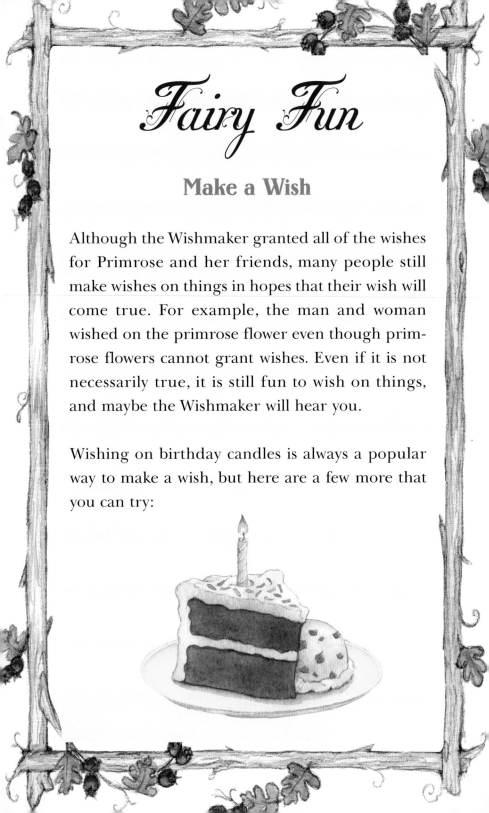

Eyelashes: When an eyelash falls and lands on your cheek, you or a friend may take it off and hold it on the tip of your finger. Make a wish and then blow the eyelash so that it flies away.

Necklaces: If you are wearing a necklace with a clasp and the necklace has turned so that the clasp is now in the front, your friend may move the clasp to the back while making a wish.

Shooting Star: Whenever you see a shooting star, make a wish!

Dandelions: When a dandelion flower goes to seed and becomes white and fluffy, you can make a wish as you blow the seeds away. If you can do it in one breath, your chances of the wish coming true are stronger.

Memory Game

Primrose is a thinker fairy and is very good at remembering clues and solving mysteries. In order to be a good detective, you must have a good memory. Try playing this game with your friends to test your memory. The more times you play this game, the better your memory will become!

What you will need:
- Seven or eight small toys and trinkets
- Space to lay out your items (a table, tray, or the floor will do)
- Bed sheet or piece of fabric large enough to cover all the items
- Stopwatch or timer
- Paper and pen or pencil for each person playing

First, without your friends seeing, gather small trinkets such as a keychain, a nail file, a button, a jellybean, a paperclip, a small toy, a rock, or a feather. These are just examples of items you can use, but you can use anything you find around your room, your house, or your yard. As your memory skills increase, you can add more items.

Place all the items on the floor, on a table, or on a tray and cover it with the bed sheet. When your friends are ready, lift the sheet off the items for everyone to see. They will have sixty seconds to study all the items on the floor and try to remember them. Use your stopwatch or timer to determine when a minute has gone by.

After one minute, cover the items again. Give each of your friends a piece of paper and a pen or pencil. They must now write down everything they can remember, but only give them three minutes to do so. Tell them to write as many details as they can remember. For example, if there is a button on the table, can your friends remember what color it was and whether it was round or square shaped?

When three minutes are done, tell them to stop writing and take the bed sheet off the items again. See who got the most items right and who remembered the most details. Try playing with different items and different time limits.

You can play a simple version of this game wherever you are—even if you are by yourself. All you need to do is look at an object near you, study it for a minute, and then close your eyes. See if you can remember exactly what it looks like.

Cranberry Garland

The Fairy Circle took place under a blackthorn tree that was decorated with bewitched cranberries that were glowing like lanterns. Although you probably cannot make cranberries magically glow, you can make your own cranberry garland that will be a wonderful treat for birds and squirrels, especially in the winter.

What you will need:
    Sewing needle
    Thread
    Cranberries
    Popcorn

Ask an adult to help thread the needle with a large length of thread and make a knot at the end. Push the sewing needle through a piece of popcorn so the thread goes through the popcorn like a bead on a necklace. Then push the sewing needle through a cranberry. (Be careful, needles are sharp. You may need an adult's help with this.) Continue to repeat this pattern until you have a long strand of popcorn and cranberries on the thread.

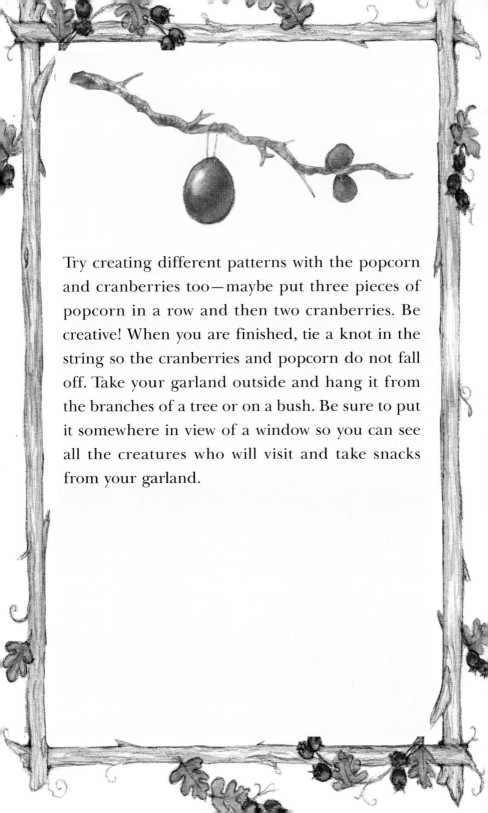

Try creating different patterns with the popcorn and cranberries too—maybe put three pieces of popcorn in a row and then two cranberries. Be creative! When you are finished, tie a knot in the string so the cranberries and popcorn do not fall off. Take your garland outside and hang it from the branches of a tree or on a bush. Be sure to put it somewhere in view of a window so you can see all the creatures who will visit and take snacks from your garland.

FAIRY FACTS

A Gargoyle Named Dedo

Throughout history, most gargoyles were sculpted to look as scary and mean as possible, so they could effectively frighten away evil spirits. However, a nun living in France during the time the Notre Dame Cathedral was being built decided to break with tradition. She secretly carved a small, sweet-faced gargoyle with pointy ears and crossed toes to place atop the new cathedral. Her creation remained undiscovered for many years until a young boy, lost high in the building, stumbled from a ledge and fell onto the roof. He rolled right down the steep rooftop and into the arms of Dedo, which proved that one of the smallest and most loveable gargoyles ever created could still be a very good protector.

Snowglobes

Sometimes called waterglobes, snowglobes are collectible knickknacks believed to have originated in France in the 1800s. Featuring scenes such as the Eiffel Tower in winter, they are still a popular souvenir of travelers to that country. Over the years, snowglobes have been made out of both glass and plastic, and the snow inside has been made from a variety of things such as sand, soap flakes, and small pieces of plastic. In addition to being beautiful, snowglobes are also functional and are often used as paperweights and for advertising. A snowglobe even takes center stage in the famous movie *Citizen Kane*.

Evening Primroses

Evening primroses are wildflowers that grow in many parts of North America. They can be either yellow or pink and are sometimes referred to as buttercups. The different varieties of primroses range greatly in height, from as short as five inches to as tall as five feet. In some parts of the country, the flowers open only in the evenings, which is how they got their name. In addition to being beautiful and fragrant, primrose plants have long been used for both food and medicinal purposes.

Inside you is the power to do anything™

The Fairy Chronicles

. . . the adventures continue

Cinnabar and the Island of Shadows

A shadow is a person's closest companion. Shadows protect and guide the humans they are attached to. But what if you were born without a shadow?

Madam Toad paused before she continued. "Human shadows are unlike any other shadows on earth. They are much different from animal, mountain, plant, cloud, insect, and building shadows. For starters, human shadows are much more complex. And they are the only shadows that are magically constructed. Human shadows are manufactured by shadowmakers on the Island of Shadows, and are delivered to children shortly after their births by hawks that work for the shadowmakers.

"Today, Mother Nature has discovered that seven children in various countries of the world have not received their shadows."

And so Cinnabar, Mimosa, Dewberry, and Spiderwort must travel to the Island of Shadows, confront the King and Queen of that remarkable place, discover what happened to these seven shadows, and, worst of all, find out if there might be someone or something behind it all!

Come visit us at fairychronicles.com

Mimosa and the River of Wisdom

Life is full of difficult choices. One of the hardest is having the power to help someone you love and not being able to. In such a situation, what would you do?

As they sat on the bed together, Mimosa sighed and tried to word her thoughts carefully. Periwinkle pulled her long dark hair back into a ponytail, clasping it with a stretchy hair tie, as she watched her friend's face closely, waiting for her to speak.

After a few moments, Mimosa sighed again, then finally said, "I'm really worried about my mom. She has tried so hard to quit smoking, but she can't. I want to help her."

"What do you mean, help her?" asked Periwinkle hesitantly.

"Well…" said Mimosa. "You know…a little fairy help."

"But you can't!" Periwinkle cried loudly. She glanced at the door and lowered her voice. "You know that we can't use fairy magic to solve personal problems. You could lose your fairy spirit."

Mimosa is one of the kindest, most courageous fairies in the world. But this is the hardest choice she has ever had to make. Should she use magic to help her mom even if it is forbidden? Should she risk losing her fairy spirit to do this?

Come visit us at fairychronicles.com

Luna and the Well of Secrets

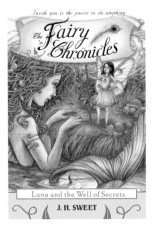

Three bat fairies have been kidnapped and taken to the Well of Secrets. To make matters worse, the Well of Secrets is the doorway to Eventide, the Land of Darkness!

"There must be extremely powerful magic involved to snatch fairies from three completely different parts of the world all in one day."

Madam Toad's face wore a puzzled expression as she continued. "And the reason only bat fairies were abducted is unknown..."

Luna, Snapdragon, Firefly, and Madam Finch are sent to the Well to discover why. Once there, they discover a Dark Witch imprisoned in a mirror, only able to come out for twelve minutes every twelve hours. Then a Light Witch arrives and the fairies have to make a choice. Who do they trust? Which one is good and which one is evil? Will they defeat the right witch without destroying the balance between light and dark?

This may be the most dangerous fairy mission ever!

Come visit us at fairychronicles.com

Dewberry and the Lost Chest of Paragon

In Dewberry's constant quest to obtain more knowledge, she uncovers the Legend of Paragon, an ancient ruler, and his three marshals— Exemplar, Criterion, and Apotheosis. Dewberry enlists the aid of her friends, Primrose and Snapdragon, in seeking the Lost Chest of Paragon, rumored to contain a great gift of ancient and powerful knowledge, one she hopes to share with all of mankind.

But when the chest is found, a catastrophe occurs, one so powerful that even fairy magic is nowhere near strong enough to fix the problem. But it was Dewberry's relentless search for knowledge that caused this disaster in the first place. She will have to do everything she can to make it right again...

Moonflower and the Pearl of Paramour

Henry, a brownie prince, loves the fairy named Rose. Forty years ago, a bitter wizard cursed them to be forever apart and forever silent. Rose is trapped in a magic painting and Henry is trapped in a book. Neither can leave their prisons, nor speak a single word, or the other will die.

But every seventy-two years, the Wishing Star of Love appears for nine days only, and when wished upon, it can lead the wisher to Paramour, the Goddess of Love. With the help of the Goddess's magic pearl, there is a way to set the cursed couple free. Since Moonflower is the Fairy of Love, she will lead the mission to rescue Henry and Rose. Can Moonflower and her friends reach Henry and Rose in time or will the couple be imprisoned forever?

The adventures don't end here!

Come visit us at
www.fairychronicles.com

for even more fairy magic and fun!

- Become a Fairy Chronicles member
- Upload your own fairy drawings
- Read about all of the *Fairy Chronicles* adventures—and get sneak peeks of the next books
- Meet each fairy and learn more about your favorite characters
- Help protect Mother Nature with cool recycling activities and ideas
- Check out the online Fairy Handbook as well as trivia, recipes, poems, and crafts
- Download special bookmarks, computer graphics, and more free stuff
- Send your friends *Fairy Chronicles* e-cards

And much more!

About the Author

J. H. Sweet has always looked for the magic in the everyday. She has an imaginary dog named Jellybean Ebenezer Beast. Her hobbies include hiking, photography, knitting, and basketry. She also enjoys watching a variety of movies and sports. Her favorite superhero is her husband, with Silver Surfer coming in a close second. She loves many of the same things the fairies love, including live oak trees, mockingbirds, weathered terra-cotta, butterflies, bees, and cypress knees. In the fairy game of "If I were a jellybean, what flavor would I be?" she would be green apple. J.H. Sweet lives with her husband in South Texas and has a degree in English from Texas State University.

About the Illustrator

Ever since she was a little girl, Tara Larsen Chang has been captivated by intricate illustrations in fairy tales and children's books. Since earning her BFA in Illustration from Brigham Young University, her illustrations have appeared in numerous children's books and magazines. When she is not drawing and painting in her studio, she can be found working in her gardens to make sure that there are plenty of havens for visiting fairies.